THE GUEST OF HONOR
BY
STACY-DEANNE
VENUS RAY

Readers: Thanks so much for choosing my book! I would be very appreciative if you would leave reviews when you are done. Much love!

Email: stacydeanne1@aol.com
Website: Stacy's Website [1]

---

1.   https://www.stacy-deanne.com/

Facebook: Stacy's Facebook Profile[2]
Twitter: Stacy's Twitter[3]

To receive book announcements subscribe to Stacy's mailing

list: Mailing List[4]

---

2.   https://www.facebook.com/stacy.deanne.5

3.   https://twitter.com/stacydeanne

4.   https://stacybooks.eo.page/cjjy6

NOTE TO READERS:

Thanks for picking up this book. The Sex in the Wild West Series is a historical interracial erotic short story series featuring black women and white men couples. Each book stands alone. This means that you don't have to read them in any specific order! If you enjoy this story then make sure to check the webpage dedicated to the series: CLICK HERE[5]

On this page you will see the books released as well as books that are upcoming so you can preorder. You can also keep up with the series on its Amazon series page under Stacy-Deanne or Venus Ray.

---

5. https://www.stacy-deanne.com/sexwildwest.html

IMPORTANT: You can also sign up for the *Sex in the Wild West Series* mailing list. You will get an email whenever a new book releases! Note, if you are a subscriber to Stacy's regular mailing list then you still need to sign up for this one if you want information on this series. Stacy will not be sending mailings about this series to her existing list since these books are erotica.

Sign up here: https://stacybooks.eo.page/rd687

Enjoy!

CHAPTER ONE

Wilkerson, Montana 1895

Winona Tidwell sat in the rocking chair in her family's little log cabin, holding her breath while Doctor Vermont examined her father.

Papa Tidwell struggled, each cough sending his skinny body into a frenzy.

It tore Winona up to see her father in such a state. He'd always been the most vibrant and strongest man she'd known. He was a carpenter at one while and he'd had such strength it wouldn't have surprised her if he could've pick up a tree with his bare hands.

Winona held in her tears, but Mama stood by the couch, sniffling. She cried enough for her and Winona put together so Winona figured someone had to be strong.

But looking upon her weak father, battered with an illness he'd had for four months, she couldn't help thinking this might be the end.

Winona and her mother held their breaths as Dr. Vermont pressed the stethoscope to Papa's chest and shook his head.

"Doctor?" Mama sniffled. "How is he? How much worse has he gotten?"

"I'm sorry." He stood up straight, his rigid, pale face covered in wrinkles. "But the sickness has moved to his lungs."

"Pneumonia?" Winona asked.

"Worse." Vermont put his items back into his medical kit. "I'd guess his lungs are stricken with the cancer."

"Cancer?" Mama turned up her nose, looking at Winona for clarification. "What is that?"

"It's a disease, Mama. You can get it all over your body and it can kill sometimes."

"Too much tobacco I reckon." Vermont stood erect, holding his kit. "His lungs are so obstructed I'm surprised he can breathe at all."

Papa coughed and wretched, his brown skin held a stale, sickly hue.

"I'm sorry to say he won't make it much longer in this condition."

"Doctor, no!" Mama grabbed Vermont's arm. "Please don't say that. It must be something
you can do."

"He needs surgery and that takes money." Vermont straightened his glasses. "And ain't no need of talkin' about it because judging by this place..." He grimaced as he glanced around their rickety log cabin. "You have little to spare."

"Tell us." Winona stood. "Whatever it is, we'll pay it."

He squinted. "Eighty dollars."

"Eighty dollars?" Mama shrieked. "Oh, Lord no. That can't be right. That's months of wages."

"Eighty dollars?" Winona replayed the number in her head. "Papa's a carpenter and I'm a maid for Mr. Hudson Ryland and together we don't even make fifty dollars a month."

"Well, what do you have to sell? I could do the surgery here at the house as soon as I got the goods. You got any animals?"

"We got one horse and a mule," Verleen said. "You can have the mule."

He scowled. "That old mule that's outside? That varmint's older than I am."

"We need our horse," Winona said. "He's the only one we have now. The other died a month back."

"*Well.*" Vermont scratched the silver stubble on his chin. "What about food?"

"We barely have enough for *us*," Winona said. "If only Daddy wasn't too sick to work, he could've made you some furniture or something."

"Gotta be eighty dollars then. I'm sorry." Vermont shuffled to the door because of his limp. "That's the best I can do."

"Are there any other doctors in these parts?" Verleen asked.

"Not that take Negroes." He opened the door, sighing. "Ralph should feel at least a little better. The medicine should help with any pain, but if he doesn't get that surgery in a few weeks, well, he won't need it. Bye for now.

"No, please!" Mama ran up and grabbed him. "Please, Dr. Vermont! Have mercy on us."

"Mama." Winona took her mother. "Let the doctor go. It's nothing more he can do."

"But we can't give up." She ran to the couch and laid upon Ralph.

With his feeble body, he barely had enough to strength to pat his wife's hand.

Winona sighed, turning to the doctor. "Thanks for the help, Dr. Vermont."

He nodded. "If you get the money, I'll get to it. But I need *something*."

"We understand, Doctor." Winona grabbed the door. "Thanks for coming out this time of

night."

He glanced at her parents and sighed. "Let me know if you need anything else."

He left.

"Lord, no!" Mama was on her knees by the couch, praying with her arms up.

"Mama, praying ain't gonna fix this."

"Hush your mouth, child." She shot Winona a look of fire. "Blasphemy. God can help anything if we believe."

"Really?" Winona crossed her arms, studying her father's struggling. "You been praying all your life and bad stuff keeps happening. We need money, not prayer." She plopped back in the chair. "We gotta figure out how we gonna get it."

"The Lord is all we need." Mama stood, grabbing her apron. "It's why your father's hanging on this long. You heard Dr. Vermont. He acting like your father should've been gone."

Ralph hacked and sweated.

"Oh, my sweet, loving husband." Mama leaned over on him. "My heart aches with every cough and pain you have. I'm gonna make sure we do right by you, Ralph."

When he finally got over his coughing spell, he sat up, gaze glued on his daughter. "Wanna get... my papers done."

"What papers?" Winona asked.

"No." Mama shook her head. "Ralph, no."

"Yes, Verleen. We can't keep acting like this ain't happening." He coughed. "I'm not gonna make it another month in this shape. I wanna get my stuff in order, so you and Winona will be okay."

"No, Daddy." Winona had vowed to be strong, but hearing her daddy mention a will was too much. "I won't let you even think this way. We gonna fight this thing together. You ain't dying. Not as long as I'm here."

He coughed, clearing his throat. "You know something I don't? We got money hidden somewhere? Where we gonna get eighty dollars from?"

"I work for one of the richest men in Wilkerson." Winona stuck her head in the air. "I'll ask him to up my pay."

"Even if he did, it won't be up to eighty dollars. No." Ralph sat back, fanning his sweaty face.

"It's over for me. It's best to take care of business now. The way I'm feeling, I could expire tonight—"

"Stop it!" Winona stood. "You stop talking like this right now, Daddy. All my life, you told me to fight. It's engraved on me. You said the worse thing anyone could do is give up." She straightened her spine. "Lord knows you never did. Look at you. Fought all the odds. A Negro man born to one of the poorest colored families around. Then you came up and started your own carpentry business with *no* money. Papa, we are where we at today, living a decent living, because of you and your fightin'."

His eyes drooped.

"I'm never gonna give up. I'm gonna ask Mr. Ryland for the money straight out."

"Stupid girl. Don't go ruining a good thing for me. You lucky to have that job and he might fire you if he think you ungrateful."

"Look at my eyes, Papa." Winona bent down to him. "I will do whatever I have to, to get you the money. I ain't letting you die."

"Winona, maybe there's another way." Verleen took her daughter's hand. "You're twenty-three now. I was married to Ralph two years by the time I was your age."

Winona huffed.

"I know you've resisted it, but the time is now. Your papa need you to marry. To a good man with some money and settle down."

"Mama, in case you've missed it, there ain't no wealthy colored men in Wilkerson, Montana."

"There's Harold Payne. Remember? The one who thinks you're the prettiest girl in Wilkerson?" Verleen stroked Winona's crinkles. "He ain't white-rich, but he's the best thing next to it. Been working at the bank for years. Oh, he really wants to marry you, Winona. He can provide you a good life."

Winona crossed her arms, tossing her gaze in the opposite direction. "I said I got a plan, Mama."

Ralph coughed, struggling to stay still.

"Thought you said you'd do anything for your daddy." Verleen scoffed. "Except give up on your heathen ideals that marriage ain't what you need. Winona, no respectful woman your age, needs to be unmarried."

"Okay." She exhaled. "Let me ask Mr. Ryland first and if he refuses, I will talk to Harold."

"And you'll let him court you finally?" Verleen grabbed Winona with animated eyes. "Huh?"

"Yes." She looked at Ralph, who was laying over, trying to catch his breath. "I said I'd do anything for Papa, and I meant it."

CHAPTER TWO

On the walk to Mr. Ryland's the next morning, Winona did her best not to talk herself out of asking him for more money. What if it ended up like Ralph thought and Hudson fired her for being ungrateful? After all, he paid his servants well, even the colored ones. Many would've died to be in her shoes, working in a gorgeous mansion every day with such a sensual boss.

They had a weird dynamic, Winona and Hudson Ryland. For one, he always spoke to her in the mornings with a smile big that lit up his whole face. It wasn't a normal smile a boss gave to a servant, it flashed as if he were genuinely happy to see her every day. Then, when she'd sweep past his lounge where he read over papers, dealing with the ins and outs of the real estate company he owned, he'd look up at her and she'd look at him too. They'd hold their gaze, only breaking it when one of the other servants passed.

Speaking of the other maids, they didn't like Winona at all. They were jealous because she was so beautiful. And yes, she knew she was attractive and didn't apologize for it. She didn't agree with society forcing modesty on women. She'd never lived her life according to the way people thought she should. It started with how she dressed. Most women in Wilkerson dressed conservatively; long-sleeve dresses with high collars that went all the way to the floor like nuns and their hair in buns.

Not Winona. She had long, wavy hair thanks to her mixed grandmother on her mother's side and she wore it down, wild and free. She also wore her arms out and her dress up to her knees. Wherever she went, women hissed and frowned at how she dared to go against conviction.

It only made her want to do it more.

But she had one friend at Mr. Ryland's, Peg, another colored maid who seemed just as enthralled with Mr. Hudson Ryland as Winona. The only difference was, he didn't look at Peg the way he did Winona.

"Isn't he handsome?" Peg stood on the last step of the winding stairwell, staring into Mr. Ryland's lounge across the hall. "He gets better looking every day. Can you imagine being married to a man like that?"

"No." Winona kept sweeping. "I cannot."

"But surely you've *dreamed*." Peg tilted her head, making them dumb googly eyes again.

Her maid's uniform was all botchy on her fat rolls. She looked like biscuit dough wearing

a dress.

"I know he wouldn't want *me* in a million years, but no one can take my dreams away." Peg squealed. "How come you ain't talked to him yet? About that money?"

"Sh." Winona squinted at one of the older maids who tottered past them with her nose in the air. "I surely don't want Bet hearing and then going to Mr. Ryland and sabotaging. And if he gives me the money, and she finds out, she'll have a fit because she's been here longer than me."

"Who cares about Bet or any of them other ones?" Peg held her round waist, batting her lashes. "This is for yo' daddy. Other than asking Mr. Ryland, you'd have to marry Harold. Ugh." She shivered. "That little mousy, boring excuse of a man. It would be like a lifetime in jail to be tied to him. No, you gotta talk to Ryland." Peg swept Winona's hair off her shoulders and straightened her sleeveless top. "Now, you look breathtaking."

"Huh? Do I *wanna* look breathtaking?"

"Girl, Mr. Ryland likes you." Peg straightened Winona's skirt. "Anyone can tell by the way he looks at you. Use it to your advantage. Stick them breastesses out." Peg stuck out her sagging chest. "Stand up tall and go on in there. Make sure you do it ladylike too, so he won't miss a beat."

"I ain't wanna do it like this, Peg. Like a whore or something. I wanna be respectable."

"This is for Ralph. You need to do whatever will get you that money. And he might even wanna poke you for it too."

"Peg!" Winona covered her laugh. "Stop talking like that."

"As if you care." She grinned. "With as filthy as yo' mind is. Yo' momma ain't here, so give up the nun routine. Go." Peg pushed Winona into the hall. "And walk sexy."

Winona rolled her eyes and walked toward Hudson's office, putting more twist in her hips when she did it. "Mr. Ryland, sir?"

He looked up, his magnetic eyes shining through his square spectacles. His eyes were the same color as her daddy's whiskey.

Hudson Ryland was definitely a vision. Slick, golden hair, and tall with a lean muscular build that even his waistcoat and trousers didn't hide. He had those triangular cheekbones that made him look serious yet playfully at the same time. And those *lips*. Pink and plump. Winona had never seen such womanly lips on a man before, and it made him even more enchanting.

"Yes, Winona?" He raised his blond eyebrow. "Is there something I can do for you?"

"Mr. Ryland, sir. Uh..." She looked back and Peg stood by the stairs, signaling with her hands for Winona to continue. "Am I bothering you, sir?"

"Just looking over some papers for Ryland Real Estate." He took off his glasses. "Nothing I can't take a few minutes from. Please, sit."

Winona tipped inside and sat in the oak chair across from his desk.

"Forgive me." He clasped his hands. "But you seem distressed. Is everything all right?"

"No, sir. How could you tell?"

"You have a face that gives away your thoughts." He smiled. "It's quite remarkable."

She swallowed, butterflies filling her stomach. "My father is dying. He has the cancer in his lungs and needs surgery."

"Oh, dear." Hudson sat back, his straight forehead wrinkling under the few strands of hair that always fell on his forehead. "Winona, I'm so sorry."

"But I ain't letting him die. My daddy's my whole world. He's the backbone of our family and I don't know what me and Mama would do without him. Mr. Ryland, sir, maybe I have no right to ask this of you, but I need eighty dollars."

He gaped. "Eighty dollars?"

"I know that's a lot, but not for a man of your means. And I'm asking you if you would help me out."

"Let me get this straight." He squinted, playing with his glasses. "You expect me to *give* you eighty dollars for your father's surgery?"

She swallowed. "Yes, sir. I wouldn't ask if I didn't have to."

He sucked his lip. "I see."

"I apologize, Mr. Ryland." She leaned forward, gripping the desk. "If it wasn't life or death, I wouldn't dare ask. I didn't know what else to do. It's either your help or marry a man I don't love."

"No." He winced. "I wouldn't want you to do that, Winona. Such a vibrant and tempting young woman you are. You deserve a man who lights your heart on fire."

"Why, *yes*." Her nipples hardened. "Yes, I do."

He stared at her, rocking in the chair. "Okay. I'll give you the money."

She squealed, slapping her hand over her mouth. "I'm sorry, sir." She laughed. "But you will?

You really will?"

"Not for free, of course."

She dropped her shoulders. "Oh."

"I'm set to go to a very important party tomorrow night. Some of the town's most influential and wealthiest men will be there."

She nodded. "Yes, sir?"

"I'll give you the eighty dollars if you accompany me to the party as my date."

"W... what? Wait a minute, sir." She wriggled. "You want *me* to be your date?"

He nodded. "I do."

"But I'm colored and poor. What on earth will people think if you walked in there with me on your arm?"

He jerked forward. "They'll think I had the most beautiful, enchanting, bewitching woman in Wilkerson, hell, in all of Montana, on my arm. Colored, poor, white, green, they won't be able to deny that."

She dropped her head, her heart fluttering. "Mr. Ryland."

"You're blushing."

She touched her light-brown cheek, and it was hot to the touch. "You flatter me, sir. But I don't deserve to go to your party. I am way beneath your station."

"Don't you want the money? Besides, I have a feeling the guests will welcome you with open arms. They're in the mood for something... different."

"But I don't have anything suitable enough to wear to a party with you."

He took out his pocket watch. "I'll have the coachman take you to the dress shop. I have an account there. Get you anything you like."

"Oh *my*." She touched her stacked bosom. "Mr. Ryland, I don't know what to say."

"I can't see how you could refuse." He sat back. "You don't wanna marry that man out of obligation. And you can't get any loans around here being a Negro. I'm giving you eighty dollars to be on my arm for one night. You know how many women would kill for that honor?"

She nodded. "I can guess, sir."

"You can have that money tomorrow night, Winona. But it's up to you. Are you coming with me or not?"

"Yes!" She jumped out of the desk and took his hand. "Oh, thank you, Mr. Ryland."

He stood, squeezing her hand. "Be ready for a night to remember."

CHAPTER THREE

"Oh, my." Verleen stared at her daughter the next night as Winona overlooked herself in the one mirror they had. "Winona?"

She turned to face her mother. "I can't believe this is me." She held out the skirt of the silk white dress. "I feel like a princess, Mama."

"My baby." Verleen reached up and touched her daughter's sophisticated ringlets. "I hardly recognize you. You're so beautiful, Winona." She sighed.

"What's wrong, Mama?"

"I don't trust this at all. Mr. Ryland and this party it... it don't feel right."

"Mama, I've been working for Hudson Ryland since I was sixteen and he's been nothing but a gentleman and fair. I trust him." Winona swung back around, straightening her dress in the mirror. "I'm tickled he asked me to come to this party. I never thought this would ever happen. Hudson Ryland is a dream, Mama. Only thirty-three and one of the richest men in the country. We got a lot in common."

Verleen grimaced. "What *you* got in common with Hudson Ryland besides breathing the same air?"

"We have the same background." Winona patted the flower pin in her hair. "Hudson was poor and everything he accomplished was with blood, sweat and tears. He knows what it's like to struggle. Mama, you got the wrong picture of him."

"I just know how white men be." She shook her head. "They do anything they can to take advantage. He knows your daddy needs that operation, so you in a dangerous position, Winona. You think you just going to a party? Wake up, girl. That white man got something up his sleeve and by God, I hope you're prepared for it."

"Well, Mama, I'm a grown woman now." Winona rubbed her embellished bodice. "I can take care of myself. Plus, what are *you* doing to help Papa?"

Verleen gasped, lips shaking.

"Oh, Mama." Winona hugged her. "I'm sorry! I didn't mean that. Please forgive me."

"No, you right." Much shorter than her daughter, Verleen sobbed into Winona's bosom. "I ain't done nothing but cried."

"That's not true." Winona held her mother's face. "Mama, you're the rock. You give Papa

strength to go on another day."

Ralph coughed and wheezed from the other room.

"Don't worry." Winona kissed Verleen's forehead. "I'm gonna get this money tonight, Mama. And everything will be all right."

"I love you, baby."

"You and Daddy moved heaven and earth to take care of me all these years. It's my turn to

do the same."

****

Squeezed up against Hudson in his luxury carriage while the coachman drove, Winona's heart pounded like thunder. Hudson scared the dickens out of her, but he made her wanna throw caution to the wind and do anything he told her to. That was dangerous, since she was so desperate to get that money. If he was as smart as she knew he was, he'd take advantage. After all, he didn't get this rich and successful by not seizing on any opportunity that might benefit him.

"You look *ravishing*." He raised an eyebrow, looking dapper in his black suit. "Are you nervous? Please don't be. You'll enjoy this night. I promise."

"Where are we going?" Winona noticed a ways back that they'd escaped the valleys of Wilkerson and was now on the outskirts. "Are we out of town?"

He just kept that mischievous grin. "The party is at a friend's. Winona, I want you to enjoy this night and it's best you don't ask too my questions."

She batted her eyes.

"Relax and not worry so much, okay?"

"Kind of hard not to worry when I don't know where I'm going."

The clop of the horse's hooves against the gravel made her more nervous. It magnified the gravity of this moment. She realized then, she didn't really know Hudson Ryland outside of being his maid. She knew his business and how he got rich, but hadn't been around him alone like this.

What if she'd misjudged him and he was really dangerous? Could this be a setup for something sinister?

"Winona?" He placed his large gloved hand on hers. "Stop worrying, okay? I'm doing this to help you and you'll have fun. Don't you want your father to have that operation?"

"Yes, sir."

"Well, relax." He squeezed her hand, the leather of his glove sending chills through her. "Everything will be all right, but you gotta trust me for this to work. Do you?"

Of course she trusted him. She was out of town in his carriage, with *his* coachman, and no way back on her own.

She had no choice but to trust him.

****

Seeing the enormous mansion didn't ease Winona's nerves any because it looked like something Satan would've stayed in. The building was just a black outline, blending into the darkness. The only distinct feature was the tall peaks that stabbed the sky. Other than that, no movement, no sound, and no sign of life.

"You know where to go," Hudson told the coachman.

The coachman nodded and directed the horse to the back of the mansion.

Winona leaned up. "Why are we going to the back?"

"I told you to calm down." Hudson opened the door of the carriage, hopped out, and held out his hand to her. "My lady?"

Holding her breath and second-guessing coming with him, Winona accepted his hand and got out of the carriage.

Hudson unlocked the back door and pulled Winona inside.

It looked like some kind of cellar.

Gray.

Hollow.

Hudson led her through the halls, each step echoing.

Just when Winona was about to pass out from nerves, they came to a brighter hallway with

portraits and golden fixtures. The floors were so shiny you could eat off them.

It was so quiet. Too quiet for a party to be going on.

Hudson pulled her into the ballroom, a giant space highlighted with crystal, gold, and glamour.

The room was so white. A blinding white. White that hurt your eyes if you stared at the walls too long.

Winona was more concerned with the scene: no food, no music, and no *women*.

Just five men in luxurious black suits with black masks that showed only their lips and chin.

They stood side-by-side with their hands clasped in front of them, no amusement in their faces.

The men seemed around Hudson's age so in their 30s. They were all fit with athletic bodies and though she couldn't see their entire faces, she could tell they were all handsome. One thing that stuck out was they were all clean-shaven, like Hudson, when most men in Wilkerson had at least a mustache.

They all had those same leather gloves on Hudson wore. The only way to distinguish them was their hair. The tallest one had raven black curls. Another man had straight brown hair to his shoulders. The other men had short brown hair, but Hudson was the only blond.

Winona decided she'd refer to them as numbers. The curly-haired one would be One. The longer-haired man would be Two, and the others: Three, Four and Five.

"Is this her?" the curly-haired one asked.

"Yes." Hudson smiled at Winona. "She's the one."

"What one?" Winona asked. "Hudson, what's going on?"

"Look around, darling." He spread out his arms. "You are the guest of honor."

She gaped.

"It's your party." Hudson kissed her hand. "And we're going to have fun in ways you never

dreamed. Then when it's over, you get the money for your father's surgery. Fine arrangement, hmm?"

"This is a sex party?" She gaped at the motionless men. "No, sir. I can't do this. I can't!" She dashed to the doorway.

"All right," Hudson announced. "It's, of course, your decision. We wouldn't dare force you to do something you didn't wanna do."

She held her breath as she turned to face him.

"But you *want* to do this, don't you, Winona?" Hudson swaggered to her as the other men just looked. "I know who you are inside, Winona. You're not like these other women, raised to be these prim and delicate flowers. You wanna let loose. Go against society's convictions. Make your own rules, hmm?" Wrinkles sprouted around his eyes. "I'm the same way, and so are our friends." He pointed to the men. "These are some of the richest and most successful men in Wilkerson. Do you know how many women would kill for this chance, Winona?"

She looked at the men, her mouth watering with curiosity.

"To be wanted, at the same time, by men who women only dream of?" Hudson said. "And tonight, we all want *you*, Winona." He put his finger on her lips. "Only you. Can you walk away from that, Winona? Especially when your father's time is running out?"

Hudson should've been ashamed of trying to manipulate her by using her father, but that's the man he was and she couldn't expect him to change.

Winona walked to the men, looking each of them over. Her nipples swelled into sensitive beads. Just them rubbing against her corset was too much to take.

The men definitely excited her, each and every one. Especially Hudson. She'd wanted him since she first got that job. And he was dead on when he said she didn't live by society's rules and that she was so sick of hiding the woman she wanted to be.

It was the danger that attracted her. The *edge*. The unpredictability.

And that's what Hudson had presented before her tonight.

How in the hell could she ever think of leaving?

CHAPTER FOUR

"The rules are up to you," Hudson said. "If there is anything you want us to do, tell us. If there is anything you don't like or you want to stop, we will. We will never abuse your boundaries because pleasuring you is the most important thing."

She nodded, and it seemed to be all the permission Hudson needed because he pulled her into his brawny arms and French-kissed her, moving his tongue all around her mouth and hitting every spot. She didn't know she had so many nerves on her tongue.

"Mm." He went faster, smacking and slurping. "Your mouth tastes so good. I can't wait to taste the rest of you." He got a chair from the huge snack table, set it behind Winona, and shoved her into it.

Funny how she wasn't half as nervous now as she'd been in the carriage. She kept her eyes on the observant men who stood quietly, some already sporting enormous erections in their trousers.

Hudson pushed up her dress and yanked down her drawers.

Winona's anxiety went back to a 9 because it kicked in that she was about to lose her virginity to Hudson and five strange, yet incredibly rich and power men who she couldn't even recognize.

But her need for pleasure halted her apprehension as Hudson licked his finger and eased it up and down inside her labia. Soon, his tongue replaced his finger, and he licked her delicately to where she barely felt it but it sent her senses into overdrive.

Winona writhed in the chair, rocking and moaning. She couldn't ignore the embarrassment she felt as the men watched her, but that was also part of the excitement. This fantasy was more than she'd ever dreamed. She'd wanted to fuck Hudson since she first saw him. Who wouldn't? But this might be her only chance in life to taste what all these super men offered and she wouldn't let a little fear get in the way.

Hell no.

Hudson growled while sucking on her puckered clit.

"Yes." Despite trying to remain ladylike while her boss ate her pussy, she learned the biggest lesson about pleasure: you couldn't control how your body reacted.

Her mind tried to keep things rational, not move in too quickly while her body was ready to have all men inside of her at once if possible.

Hudson moved her dress out of his way and stuck his tongue into her snatch, moaning and groaning as if he were having the best meal of his life. "Get some of this." He munched. "Come on."

The curly-haired man and the one with the long hair, One and Two, dropped to their knees beside Hudson and Winona wondered what the hell this was.

"We're gonna suck your toes." One said, his mask rising as he smirked.

One and Two unlatched her little silver dress shoes and slipped off her stockings.

Hudson kept sucking her, his head moving so fast between her legs she wondered if it would spin off.

One and Two slipped her big toes in their mouths at the same time. And Winona couldn't describe the feeling. It reminded her of the joy she got from eating ice cream, opening Christmas gifts, and playing games with her parents on her birthdays all at the same time.

"Oh." She rubbed her tits through her dress and corset. "Yes, oh."

She'd seen nothing as beautiful as having one man lick her clit while the others sucked on her toes like slaves. Her own personal sex slaves who had to do what she wanted.

"Yes!" She leaned back, spreading her legs wider.

One and Two moaned, moving her big toe in and out of their mouths.

They switched to the other toes, wetting them and licking in between, hitting the nerves.

"Ooh, like that. Ah." Winona held onto the chair. "Oh, don't stop! Yes. Keep sucking my toes."

Hudson felt great on his own, but the toe sucking was absolutely mind-blowing.

"God, yes!" Winona looked at the other three men and they walked toward her, picking up her cue.

Three stood behind her and pulled her bodice down and unbuttoned her corset.

Winona's caramel bosom plopped into his large, gloved hands.

He massaged them, circling the bottoms of her heavy breasts in his soothing palms, then pinching her nipples between two fingers.

Four and five grabbed her hands, removed her gloves, and sucked on her fingers.

"Oh, God." Winona squirmed, sweat beading up on her face. "Yes, oh."

With the finger sucking, it wasn't the feeling that made it so amazing but seeing the men do it. Nothing more exciting than having these rich men do all she could handle.

"Let's lay her down now," Hudson said.

Two of the men helped a woozy Winona to the floor and laid her flat. She'd forgotten about that flower pin in her hair until Two snatched it off, releasing her lengthy waves.

"I'm gonna get underneath you now," Hudson said.

She leaned up on her elbows. "What?"

The others snickered as Hudson laid on his back and wiggled himself underneath Winona to where her ass was on his face.

Winona shrieked as his thick tongue slipped into her asshole. "Oh, wow. Yes!" She rode on his face. "Oh, God!"

Five got beside Hudson and, for the love of all Winona knew, he started eating her pussy! Right there while Hudson was eating her ass.

Simultaneously, they sucked and licked, the men's heads keeping the same rhythm.

"Oh, I can't take it!" Chills shot through her toes. "I can't take it!"

Three pulled his pants down, massaging his thick, blushing cock. "May I fuck your tits?"

Winona lay flat again, her tongue wagging so much she couldn't talk. She only managed a brief nod.

Three smiled and sat on top of her chest.

Winona kept her eyes on his gloved hands as he caressed her tits, and then sucked her

nipples.

How on earth would he fuck her breasts?

Was that even *possible*?

"Relax." Three's eyes lit up as he spit a glob between her tits, held them together like two pieces of bread on a sandwich, and slipped his warm cock in between them.

"Oh my God." Winona gaped in pure shock as this man fucked her titties like it was her ass.

"Yes." He leaned back with his eyes closed. "Yes, right there."

Winona just stared at him with her mouth open wondering what these men would come up with next.

She couldn't fathom she'd ever need more than this. Then her mind started wandering to what happens beyond this moment? With her and Hudson? Was this a onetime thing? With the others, she'd be fine with that, but tonight gave her hope that he saw her as more than his maid.

That he was using her father's sickness as an excuse to be with her.

Hudson squeezed her ass, his tongue prodding her asshole masterfully.

The other men felt great, magnificent, but not one of them made her body float through the air or her emotions tumble the way Hudson did.

They'd broken the barrier. Pandora had opened her box.

No matter what happened tonight, Winona couldn't go back to how things were.

She stared at the lanterns hanging from the ceiling as Three made one final jerk.

"Ah!" He wriggled his shaft, covering her with creamy, white pearls. "Oh, yes." He shuddered as if he'd been struck by lightning.

Hudson and Five stopped just before Winona was about to burst and already she was sick of being teased.

"Please." She sucked her lip. "Don't stop."

"Don't worry, darling." Hudson opened her legs wide enough where he and Five could get

between them. "We're just getting started."

CHAPTER FIVE

"Ooh." Winona bounced, grabbing the men's heads while their tongues fought over her cunt. "Yes, God!"

Five held her thigh so tightly he left a bruise, but she loved it. She craved whatever this night had in store.

"God." Hudson licked her like a pro. "You taste like honey."

He stopped to take a breath and Five took over.

It was weird how tongues could feel so different. Hudson's was soft and wide, like pressing a big soggy sponge against her clit.

Five's tongue was drier and lumpier, but his skills beat out the weird texture.

They moved aside and allowed Three and Four to get a taste and boy did they ever.

Three started off slowly, gulping as he drank her wetness. Then Four wiggled on in there, spreading her lips wide and licking along the sides.

"Yes." Winona jumped upright. "Like that. Ooh! Yes. Lick it. I... I'm gonna burst!"

The tingle in her tits. The chill trickling down her spine. The heat in the back of her thighs. The pounding filling her pussy.

This was it. Virgin or not, Winona knew she was about to do that thing that made people scream their throats off when making love.

"Mm!" She held their gyrating heads as the men battled to bring her to the finish line first. "Go on." She threw her legs in the air. "Ah, yes! Keep going. Oh, ah!" Winona creamed until Three and Four looked like someone had doused their faces with warm milk.

They looked at each other and laughed.

Winona burst into laughter herself feeling no need to be embarrassed at this point.

Yet, Winona still hadn't gotten her fix.

Hudson Ryland.

She'd had him one way. Now she couldn't leave without having him another.

She looked up at Hudson and lay back down, batting her eyes.

He walked up and the other men moved back, giving Winona and Hudson their moment.

Seemed like hours passed that Winona and Hudson just looked at each other, signaling their

desperate attraction for each other. Her doubt flew out the window then. The way he looked at her,

the sparkle in his eyes and the parting of his lips told her he cared about her. She didn't need to ask.

Hudson slowly undid his trousers. By the time they were down to his ankles, Winona was already in heaven.

She didn't know what to expect, but seeing his cock for the first time stole her breath away.

Girth.

Long, hard and wide, with deep ridges. Balls plump and smooth.

"Touch me."

Her hand shot out as if his dick had commanded its presence. She didn't know what she was doing. She just explored him like she always wanted to. Stroking and rubbing, she became overwhelmed she was finally touching a man.

"How does it feel?" Hudson whispered. "Touching my dick?"

Nothing she said could've described the feeling, so she answered with a quick lick that made him twitch. She did it again, loving having such control over this experienced lover. A couple of more licks and she got the courage to put his entire cock into her mouth, tasting his salty, bitter flesh.

"Yes." Hudson closed his eyes, his abdomen swelling as she pushed her lips back and forth. "Ooh, Winona."

"I want you inside me." She smacked when she released his cock. "It's what I've wanted since I met you."

He knelt in front of her, naked with the body of Adonis, and finally removed her disheveled dress.

She'd forgotten she had it on.

The others were naked now and stroking themselves. The only thing in place were their

masks.

"What do you want?" Hudson whispered.

"I want you to fuck me." Winona lay over. "And never stop."

Smirking, Hudson stroked her legs and gave her cunt more of his masterful mouth. Because the men had done a great job of warming her up, Hudson entered her with ease.

She flinched at the slight stinging, but it went away as soon as they started thrusting.

"Hold on." Hudson sat flat on his romp and pulled her into his lap. "I like it better this way."

He slid back inside of her. "Oh, you feel so good, Winona. I've wanted you for so long. But I was afraid to make a move."

"You?" She bounced, on his lap. "But nothing scares you, Hudson. Surely not me."

"That's... where you're wrong. Ah." He squeezed her ass. "I was scared because I felt something for you I haven't felt in a long time and I didn't know how to tell you."

She held onto his shoulders, fighting the build up in her cunt.

"Part of it was society. I was afraid of how they'd judge me. Scared of what they thought." He looked toward the others, who were moaning from intense pleasure. "But I'm not scared anymore. I want you, Winona. I want you!"

"Oh." One bent over as if he were about to dumb a wad on the floor within seconds.

"Ooh." Two sucked his lips, stroking his dick until it turned red.

Three, Four and Five filled the room with their moans as well.

"Do you want me, Winona?" Hudson grunted.

"Yes." She rode him. "I want you more than anything.'

The others surrounded them and with Winona's silent permission, they laid her down again, but this time, they took turns inside of her and while one man got his fill, the others stayed creative by doing other things to make her come even faster each time.

She wrapped her legs around whoever at the moment and just listened to her heart pounding, skin slapping, her desperate screams and the men's overlapping moans.

She reached out, grabbing different men by different body parts.

A hairy chest that felt like silk. Someone's velvety pubic hair rubbed against her cunt with force. Her fingers stroking soft black curls. Someone's thick sideburns rubbing against her thighs as the men took turns eating her again.

The musky odor grew with each stroke, overtaking the smell of different colognes and luxurious leather and richness. She even smelled the light mint of cachous on someone's breath.

Intense. Confusing. Fantastic.

Just a cloud of steamy pleasure. It was all a blur.

Winona got greedy. Each time a man came inside of her, she wanted to taste him. She got wetter from the sweet flavor of her own pussy.

They went on and on and on. Hands, touching and grabbing Winona as if they couldn't get enough. She felt like an animal being devoured, but with pleasure instead of violence.

Wrapped up in so much passion, she didn't know who was doing what and didn't care as long as they didn't stop.

And they didn't.

Not until she finally succumbed to the everlasting, mind-bending bliss cascading through her body.

THE END

SAMPLE OF SEX IN KENYA: CHAPTER ONE

(2018)

"Will you stop bitching every five minutes?" Adam Jessup scrolled through his phone while he and Vette Marlon waited at the baggage carousel for their luggage. "Since we left the US, you've been complaining about everything."

"I'm hot." She fanned her face with a pamphlet, her curly yellow hair stuffed underneath her straw hat. "It's like four hundred degrees in this place. God. And why is everyone staring at us? Because we're white?"

Adam exhaled, checking the hotel reservations on his phone. "Maybe because you're being a bitch."

"Excuse me?" She moved aside as people grabbed their luggage. "You're the one with an attitude the whole time."

"That's because you complain about every damn thing." Adam stuffed his phone in his pocket. "Of course it's hot. It's Africa!"

Since he'd been a child, 30-year-old Adam's mother always told him that good people got their wish. So after all these years of living a squeaky-clean life, being an upstanding citizen and going to church even when his friends made fun of him for missing all the Sunday games, he'd finally made it to Africa.

The Global Health Foundation had sent him to Nairobi, Kenya to oversee a shipment of supplies to a local food bank. After six years of volunteering with the GHF, they'd tasked him with his first unsupervised mission and it made him damn proud.

Too bad he'd come with loud ass Vette Marlon who'd complained since they gotten off the plane. It would take a hell of a lot for Adam to hold his tongue on this trip.

They grabbed their bags from the carousel.

"This is for charity." Adam huffed as they walked toward the glass doors with people sliding in and out of them. "Think about the reason we're here."

"I don't wanna be here." Vette hurried alongside him in flip-flops. "I hate this place already. It's so hot I can't even see. Look at me, Adam." She threw out her white arm, the color of a snowstorm. "I'm paler than the average white person. I'm fuckin' translucent. You know what this sun will do to my skin? I got on five bottles of sunblock and that ain't even helping."

People gaped at Vette as she and Adam passed.

"Everyone's looking at you," Adam said. "Stop acting like a moron."

"So I'm making this up?" Her sandals clacked against the tile.

"It's not

hot to you?"

"We're from Florida, remember?" Adam huffed as they exited the airport. "You should be used to the heat... God damn." The sun punched Adam in the face as soon as they got outside. "Jesus." He slipped on his shades.

"Uh-huh." Vette folded her arms, thin mouth in a permanent scowl. "So who's complaining now?"

"Shit, my cap's in my damn luggage."

Vette grinned. "Want my hat? Sike."

"Whatever." He wiggled his toes in his Nikes. "I got on sneakers and thick socks and the sun is still burning my feet. And you got on flip-flops?" Adam looked around, noticing they seemed to be the only ones sweating and complaining. "The cement's burning through my shoes. I ain't never experienced heat like this."

"Please, *please*." Vette squeezed her hands together. "Tell me it isn't too late to go back."

"Let's find a cab, get to the hotel and out of this heat."

She saluted him. "Aye, aye, Captain!"

He mumbled, rolling his eyes.

CHAPTER TWO

If Adam expected Vette to chill once they got into the air-conditioned cab, he was wrong. She complained about the smell of the cab and that there wasn't enough room in the back to stretch her legs. But Adam refused to let these inconveniences bother him. No. He kept his mind on the sights. He tried to guess how many people there were in this little block alone, but there had to be hundreds. People walking on top of each other, in the middle of the street, through traffic. A car meant shit to them.

Brown and black ashy feet in dusty sandals. People yelling and cars honking. Bumper-to-bumper traffic. Long, ragged streets. Hustlers in old T-shirts and faded jeans looking to score off dumb tourists.

"Look at 'em." Vette took off her hat, looking around with narrow, cynical green eyes. "Like roaches."

"Shut up." Adam nudged Vette with his elbow.

The driver peeked at her from the corner of his eye.

"For some reason you thought you being in charge of this trip meant you're in charge of *me*." Vette nudged Adam back. "Well, you're not. Yeah, I said it," she yelled for the driver to hear. "They're like roaches. Walking all on top of each other. All in the streets like they don't know how to act. This isn't acceptable where we come from—"

"*Watch* it." Adam grabbed her wrist. "You don't want to sound racist do you, Vette?"

She rolled her eyes.

It wasn't that Adam was surprised. Everyone knew Vette was a racist bitch, but Adam had hoped she'd have *some* decorum for the sake of decency.

"Hey it's okay." The bright-eyed, purple-skinned driver snickered, rolling a toothpick in his mouth. "Let the lady talk. It don't bother me. She's showing her ignorance."

24

"Ignorance?" The imprint of Vette's bouncing breasts showed through her sweaty T-shirt. "Ain't that the pot calling the kettle black? And I mean *blacker* than *black*."

"Shut the fuck up!" Adam grabbed her arm. "I'm warning you."

"Get off me!" She struggled to free herself. "Who do you think you are?"

"I'm sorry, sir," Adam told the driver. "Believe me, I wouldn't have brought her if I didn't have to."

Vette scoffed. "No I was the only one who would come with you to this place. Let go of me, Adam." She hit him and he turned her loose.

"Is she drunk?" the driver asked.

Adam plopped back in the seat. "It's the one time she needs to be."

"A drink." Vette's eyes lit up. "That's what I need." She dug in her

purse and pulled out a tiny bottle of vodka.

Adam grabbed it before she took a swig. "What the fuck are you doing? I said no alcohol on this trip, Vette."

"Excuse me." She snatched the bottle back, batting her long lashes. "Are you my daddy? I'm twenty-eight-years-old. I can drink whenever I fucking want to."

He took the bottle again. "I'm not gonna have you sloppy drunk and acting like a fool on this trip. No drinking." He stuffed the bottle in his pocket. "You settle down."

She crossed her arms, smacking her lips.

"We're gonna go to the hotel, refresh, get to the food bank and help with the shipment. Drop the attitude, Vette. I'm warning you."

"Eat me, Adam." She squinted. "Oh, I forgot. You already did."

The driver chuckled.

Adam groaned. "Bitch."

****

"Thank God we're here!" Vette plopped down on Adam's hotel bed.

"I'm glad we got rooms right next to each other. Ah." She kicked off her

shoes. "I'm drained. That flight took everything out of me."

Whenever the GHF sent volunteers on overseas assignments, they always paid for the rooms and while Adam had been stuck in some dumps before, the Foundation didn't do too shabby this time.

A multi-room suite wrapped in subtle, yellow lighting brought charm to the dreary brown walls. Sand-colored curtains made the space cozier while the chic furniture stayed true to the room's swanky integrity.

"This is pretty nice, huh?" Adam opened the intricate wooden doors of the balcony, greeted by the sticky humidity.

"Are you crazy?" Vette scoffed. "I'm dying to get out of the heat and you're going back into it?"

Adam rested on the aluminum railing, admiring the city across the horizon. "You can see everything from here. Wow, look at that pool. It's huge."

"I'll pass."

"Come on, Vette. Compared to the places the GHF has put us in, you gotta admit this is beautiful."

"It should be with all the work we do for them and for *free*, I might add."

Adam expected to find a hotel like this in ritzy Florida spots like Boca Grande or Naples, not tucked away in a quiet corner away from the rest of Nairobi.

"Did you see how the guy at the front desk was looking at us?" Vette asked.

Adam chuckled. "Everyone's been looking at us."

"Yeah, well." Vette stood, rubbing the bedspread. "I don't like it. Make sure you lock up your stuff. They'll come in our rooms and rob us blind."

"Why?" Adam scratched his arm. "Neither of us have shit. We're broker than two jokes."

"You know how they are."

He looked back at her. "Do me a favor? While we're here, keep your racist comments to yourself because I don't appreciate them."

"Racist? Come on, you've heard how they are here in Africa."

"How are *they*?"

"Please. You can be Mr. Woke all you want to, but it's just us now. Why do you think everyone warned us about the crime in this place? They didn't just make it up."

"And there's not crime in Florida?"

"Yes, there's definitely crime in Florida and look who's committing it." She stretched. "I was born in Tallahassee, and I barely recognize it now. Every sign's in Mexican. The neiGHForhoods are a mess. It wasn't like that before—"

"I don't wanna hear this shit."

"Look at California. The Mexicans took over, and it's a dump."

"Why are you even a part of the GHF with the way you are? You do realize many who need our help are not white?"

"Don't give me that. You know how they all are."

"*Who*?" he shouted.

"The blacks, the Mexicans, Muslims, name them."

"Get the fuck out of my room."

"I'm not trying to fight with you—"

"Go!" He pointed at the door. "Don't make me throw you out."

"Fine." She snatched her purse, swung it over her shoulder and twisted to the door. "I'll be in my room if you need me."

Adam rolled his eyes as he turned back to the balcony. "I won't."

"You won't? Are you sure about that?"

"More than sure, Vette." He kept his back to her, enraptured by the aroma of fruit and spices from the street markets.

"Hmm." She joined him on the balcony and stood right behind him. "You're lying." She walked her delicate fingers down his sweaty nape. "Remember our night, Adam? After the GHF Christmas party last year?"

He sighed, flinching at her touch.

"We had a moment, wouldn't you say?" She hugged him from behind. "I bet you hadn't felt that good in a long time. Remember, how upset you were that night because your wife left you? I was there, Adam." She lay against his back, squeezing his abs. "I was there when you had no one else."

CHAPTER THREE

"Vette." Adam pulled at her hands. "Leave."

"Why are you treating me this way?" she purred. "So mean and hateful with the things you say?"

"Oh, I'm not the one with the problem here." He pushed her away and faced her. "And let's not talk about who's mean and hateful."

"You enjoyed that night." She pushed curls out of her face. "You said you did."

"We were *drunk*. It was just one night when things got out of hand."

"*No*." She sucked her lip. "You wanted me. You can't deny the attraction." She tangled her fingers in his T-shirt. "Why would you want to?"

"I told you." He pushed her again. "It was a mistake. I don't have feelings for you, Vette."

"Yeah?" She lowered her stare to his crotch. "If I stayed in here long enough, you would."

"Out." He shoved her, causing her to stumble. "Go refresh or whatever so we can get to the food bank and do what they need us to do. That's why we came here, remember?"

"Fuck you." She sashayed off the balcony and grabbed her purse. "I got better things to do then hang around your stuck up ass all day."

"What?" He hurried into the room. "We're supposed to help the food bank—"

"You're so perfect and in charge, you do it."

"We have a job to do here. Why the fuck did you even sign up for this trip if you didn't want to help?"

"You're so smart, right?" She opened the door. "Guess." She left.

"Jesus." Adam shook off his frustration, because there were more important things to think about than Vette, and as he unpacked, someone knocked on his door.

"Mr. Adam?" a man beckoned with a high-pitched East African accent.

Adam recognized the voice of the front desk manager, Meshack, and answered the door. "Hello."

The giddy, yellow-skinned African with freckles dotting his face, grinned back from ear-to-ear. "Hello, Mr. Adam. I wanted to make sure you're settling in all right. Is the room sufficient for you?"

"Oh, yes it's lovely." Adam smiled, holding his waist. "Thank you. What can I do for you?"

"Well..." Meshack's sparse eyebrows danced. "It's more of what I can do for *you*." He held a lopsided grin as he raised on his tiptoes to peek over Adam's shoulder. "Is your uh, companion with you?"

"Companion?" Adam grimaced. "You mean Vette? No, she went to her room, I guess."

"Excuse me if I am prying, but are you not together?"

"Hell no." Adam shook his head. "No, no way."

"I can be of help to you then." The much-shorter man strutted inside, his name badge sitting crooked on his flabby chest. "I didn't want to share this in front of your lady friend, but we offer special 'amenities' for the gentlemen at the hotel if they're interested."

Adam squinted, closing the door. "Special amenities?"

"You know." Meshack leaned forward, eyebrow raised. "We like to make our guests' stay as pleasurable as possible."

"Ah." Adam snickered. "You're one of those hotels that hire out prostitutes for tourists?"

"Not prostitutes. *Escorts*. It goes beyond sex. She will show you around the city and spend time with you. We deal with a company and everything is safe and reputable." Meshack told Adam the name of the company. "The women are gorgeous, clean and STD-free."

Adam scratched the back of his head. "That's not really my thing—"

"Sometimes you don't know what your thing is until you try it." Meshack winked. "This is a professional service, the women are of age, they get paid fairly and are treated very well." He twisted his face. "No trafficking, drugs or abuse, no. I'd never condone anything like that. You just get the company of a beautiful woman to help you pass the time." He smiled. "Surely, you can't say no to *that*."

CHAPTER FOUR

Adam checked in with the food bank and got back to the hotel by nightfall. He stopped at Vette's room, but she didn't answer. Either she'd left or was ignoring him and though he regretted throwing her out of his room earlier, he was too exhausted for her bullshit.

Drained, Adam headed to bed when someone knocked on his door around 9 PM. He greeted a stunning African woman with a purse on her arm and a large basketful of towels, soaps, and lotions.

The escort.

Shit. He'd forgotten about her.

She smiled with the whitest teeth he'd ever seen. Cinnamon-brown eyes sparkled against her rich, chestnut-brown skin.

She slipped inside the room smelling of coconut.

Adam was 6'2 so according to where her head hit him she was at least 5'9. God had blessed her with elegant, narrow features that enthralled a man on the spot.

She sashayed to the dresser, the multicolored wrap dress massaging her sleek, thin frame. She turned and smiled at Adam. "Hujambo," which meant, "hello" in Swahili. "My name is Grace Gitau. It's nice to meet you, Mr. Jessup. I hope you are enjoying your stay in Nairobi so far."

Grace?

Adam expected some exotic African name. "Thank you." He cleared his

throat. "Nairobi's lovelier than I could imagine."

And so are you.

"This might sound stupid." He chuckled. "But I'm guessing you're the escort?"

Her tiny, triangular-shaped breasts jiggled underneath the sheer material. "Yes."

"Okay." He exhaled, rocking. "I've never done this before."

"I understand."

His loins melted at the sound of her sultry accent. "Forgive me if I'm a little nervous."

"You've been with ladies before, haven't you?"

"Of course."

She blinked. "This is no different."

"I disagree." Adam chuckled, rubbing his hair. "I've never been with a complete stranger."

"That's what makes this easier." She wiggled her shoulders. Everything she did spelled sex.

"Emotions get in the way." She smiled. "Sometimes it's best to let your mind rest and have your body take control."

He nodded. "Guess I never thought of it as so straightforward."

"It can be." Grace took off her head wrap showing him her braids in a pristine bun and then her phone rang, destroying the intimacy. "Excuse me." She rushed to the dresser and grimaced as she got her cell out of her purse. "It is nothing." She sighed. "Sorry about that."

"Everything's okay?"

"Yes." She fidgeted as she put her phone away. "What were we talking about?"

"About this uh... arrangement." Adam chuckled. "It's new to me and all."

Her phone rang again.

She huffed as she yanked the phone out again. "I apologize."

"No, it's no problem. If you need to take that I can wait—"

"No." She stabbed her finger into the phone. "I will turn it on vibrate."

"You sure everything is okay?"

"Just an overzealous client." She flashed a forced smile as she sat on the bed. "Just ignore it if it buzzes. You're enjoying the city?"

"Yes."

"What do you like about it so far?"

"Well..." Sweat beaded on the back of Adam's neck, but it wasn't from the heat. "I haven't seen any sights yet, but I like the hotel and the food is amazing. Meshack said you can show me around the city?"

"I'd love to." She looked up at him through her flirty lashes. "I'm here to make your trip as pleasurable as possible. You've paid for a good time and I plan to give it to you."

Like any other business deal, Grace showed him her ID, proving her age of twenty-eight and even presented a document showing she was healthy and free of any disease. She spelled out the rules. No kissing on the lips, no weird or outrageous sex acts, and no action without use protection. If he didn't agree, no deal.

"I'm confused," Adam said. "Why does the company not allow kisses?"

"It's not *them*, Mr. Jessup." She put the document back into her purse. "The kissing is *my* rule. I don't allow my clients to kiss me on the lips."

"Why not?"

"Because kissing is too personal."

"Hold on." He laughed. "You can have intercourse with random men but they can't kiss you?"

"These are the rules." She shrugged one shoulder. "If you don't agree I will leave."

"No, it's just I don't see why kissing is different from everything else."

"It's just a line I won't cross."

"What if I forget? I mean, when we're into it? What if I do it by accident?"

"You won't."

"How do you know?"

Her mouth rose in the corner as she smiled. "I'll remind you."

He didn't like this. Didn't like it at all. Adam loved kissing. It was his favorite part of having sex.

Shit, he paid for her, he should be able to kiss her if he wanted.

He'd accept it because the last thing he wanted was Grace leaving. And though he didn't like this no-kissing shit one bit, he would savor every moment with this African goddess. Kiss or not, she'd been the woman of his dreams before he knew she existed.

CHAPTER FIVE

Grace removed her dress and glided to Adam buck-naked with no qualms at all and unbuttoned his shirt. His heart flip-flopped like it did when that sexy doctor gave him that penis exam a few years back when he had that savage urinary tract infection.

Grace moved like a robot, undressing him without batting an eye. Her mind trained on the mission. She was the escort, but Adam worried about pleasing *her*. He was no nervous he couldn't imagine getting into his groove. What if he were so bad she canceled the arrangement and gave him a refund? Talk about embarrassing.

"Relax." She smiled.

"Have you ever been with a woman?" he blurted out, not knowing why the hell he had.

She wiggled her dainty nose. "No."

"Did I offend you?"

She laughed. "Why would I be offended?" She threw his shirt on the floor. "You'd be shocked what clients ask me." She bent down, yanking at his zipper.

"*Whoa.*" He jerked, chuckling. "You don't waste time, do you?"

Her stiff, black nipples jiggled as she removed his pants.

"You said you get a lot of weird questions from clients?"

"It comes with the territory." She stood upright. "Some think that because I'm an escort, I have no boundaries. You won't believe what some people want me to do." She held her waist, perky breasts standing at attention. "There's some very freaky people out here."

Adam clenched his dick through his underwear, imagining how her mouth would feel on it. "Anyone ever get rough with you?"

"Some have tried, but I can handle myself."

He stared at her nipples, looking like giant Hershey's Kisses.

"Sit down," she commanded.

Adam sat, and she bent down in front of him, snatching off his socks.

Here he was sitting in front of her with this big, swollen pink cock ajar in her face and she looked at it like a secretary filing papers. Of course this was a job to her, but Adam expected a smile, a moan, any acknowledgement of his blessed member. After all, this cock had sent his soon-to-be ex-wife into fits of infinite ecstasy, but Grace's aloof reaction made him wonder just how many men she'd fucked.

She fluttered her long lashes. "We're going to take a shower."

"Huh?"

"Come on." She grabbed the basket and went to the bathroom.

By the time Adam got in there she was already under the water, standing against the tile wall, staring at him. "Get in."

He swallowed, even the creases in the bend of his knees sweated.

Oh, make no mistake. He wanted to fuck her. Wanted to beat the brakes off that sweet, African punani but paying for it just felt desperate and awkward. And it didn't help that Grace looked at his dick like a scientist in a laboratory.

"You ever had sex in the shower?" she asked.

"I've had sex in lots of places."

"Ah." She raised an eyebrow. "Get a lot of women?"

"Can't complain."

He wasn't cocky but he'd never met a woman who didn't find him

attractive. So he'd never had a problem finding fuck partners and though he'd been faithful to his wife, he'd been surprised at how many women didn't give a damn he was married and tried to get a spin on his old "love rod" anyway.

Grace tilted her head. "You're a ladies man?"

"I wouldn't say *that*. I mean I don't do nothing for it to happen. Women just like me."

She grinned. "I see."

"I'm not trying to be arrogant." He chuckled, waving off his last statement. "But it's true. Just something about me I guess."

"There definitely is." Grace's stare showered his body. "You are a beautiful man, Adam. Coal-black hair and killer blue eyes. Great body."

He tingled, clearing his throat. "Thank you." He stepped under the water and grinned as the warm sprinkles tickled his nipples.

"I bet your father is so handsome," Grace said.

"I wouldn't know."

She gaped.

"Never met the man or seen one picture." He scratched his arm. "Apparently he was just some dude my mom banged after meeting him in a bar."

"I'm sorry."

"It's okay. You don't miss what you never had."

"You don't know anything about him?"

"Mom stayed tightlipped but I have heard rumors through the years that he was married when they hooked up. Either way he doesn't want nothing to do with me."

She stuck out her chin. "How do *you* know?"

"I figure if he wanted to know me he'd been around."

"But you don't know if he tried to be around you. You have no idea what happened between him and your mother. Maybe he wanted to be in your life but your mother didn't want him to be."

He shook his head. "No, no."

"How do you *know*, Adam?" She clasped his wrist. "If your mother never said the reason and you've never met the man, you're just guessing." She let him go. "Don't judge your father when you can't be sure of what's going on."

"You're right. I don't know but still, if any woman tried to keep me from my kid, I'd do all I could to see him. So that's why I think he's full of shit. Sorry I just do. Can we talk about something else?"

"Like your penis?" She chuckled as she reached out the shower and got a rag from the basket. "I like it." Grace flung him around and washed his back and shoulders.

As if he wasn't nervous enough, he got an intense cramp in the pit of his stomach and cursed himself for having that steak and onions for dinner.

Shit. Please don't fart.

He held it in until the pain subsided and his ass relaxed.

Thank God.

If he'd farted, he might've blown poor Grace back into the hallway.

"You're so tense." She kneeled while working the rag up his thighs, the aromatic soap scenting the bathroom.

She washed between his wet cheeks, massaging his asshole, his dick about to pop.

"Mm." He grabbed it with both hands.

She snickered. "Feel good?"

"Yeah." He wiggled his toes in the water. "You need to bathe me more often."

She smiled. "There you go. You're relaxing. Hold on because the fun's just beginning. Turn around."

He did, and she washed his abdomen, dragging the rag through his thick, black pubic hair.

He glared down at her, talking to her with his eyes.

Get the tip. Please, please get the tip.

She finished washing or *teasing* him and smiled. "Your turn."

"Uh, okay." Adam got a new rag out the basket.

Grace turned around and pressed her hands to the wet tile, tight little brown ass shining with water. "Take your time."

Adam glided the rag over her glossy skin, exploring every inch of her.

The shifting muscles in her back. The curve of her bony hips, the smooth, never-ending length of her creamy legs.

"How did you get into escorting?"

She glanced at him over her skinny shoulder. "Kind of personal, you think?"

"We're two strangers sharing a shower." He grinned as he turned her around, looking right into her delicious nipples. "I think we're passed subtleties."

"Just circumstances, I guess." She pursed her pouty lips, creases running through her forehead. "There aren't many options around here especially for women. You do what you need to, to survive."

"I don't buy that." He massaged her arm with the rag. "You seem like a resourceful woman. There's gotta be more you can do than this."

She raised her eyebrows. "Are you saying you have an issue with my line of work?"

"I can't complain about any occupation that puts a beautiful woman in my shower unless you're not being treated right. I hope that's not the case."

"The company I work for? Oh, no it's wonderful. Very professional place. I'm not forced to do anything I don't want. It's just like any other job. We sign contracts and are held to high standards and we even get bonuses."

"Bonuses, huh?" He pinched her cheek. "What do you have to do for these bonuses?"

She wriggled, coyly. "I'm not being abused and I can walk away at any time. I choose to do this because compared to anything else, it's one of the best ways I can make money fast to help my family. Besides, if I wasn't an escort, we'd never met."

He smirked, squeezing out the rag.

"You're different. Clients usually don't care about my life. They just get what they want and go."

"Well, I'm not like that."

"Why are you here again?"

"In Kenya?" He licked his lips as he moved the rag over her kinky pussy hairs. "I'm a volunteer with the Global Health Foundation. They sent me to check the shipment for the food bank and help them get things organized."

"That's wonderful. How did you get into that?"

"Well, my mom always instilled in me how important it is to be a good person." He fondled her pussy through the rag. "That there is always someone out there that needs a hand, and I like helping people."

"I want to move to the States. I'm working toward my Visa."

"That's great."

"Where are you from?"

"Tallahassee, Florida."

"Really?" She gushed. "I have family in Miami."

"Wow, it is a small world, huh?"

"Do you travel a lot with the Foundation?"

"I've been all over the world, but it feels different this time."

"Why?"

"I don't know." His temperature rose as he looked into her soothing eyes. "Maybe it's the company."

She smiled and after he finished washing her, she went back to work on him, stroking and teasing.

Adam struggled not to climax, but Grace just wouldn't leave his cock alone.

"Ooh." He wobbled, holding the wall. "I'm coming."

"Yes, Adam." She rubbed faster, pointing his dick to her tits. "Come now. Give it to me. I want it so bad."

"Oh. Ah!" He ejaculated, squirting thick cream right on her chest. "Ooh. Fuck. "

Grace moaned, cum hanging from her nipples. "Good *boy*."

CHAPTER SIX

"Lay down," Grace ordered Adam once they got back into the bedroom. "Put your face into the pillow."

"What are we doing?"

"Trust me. You will like it."

Adam melted every time Grace touched him, and this time was no different. He breathed into the lavender-scented pillow as she massaged him, calming every muscle. His loins raced, dick swelling into another erection.

She climbed her damp, thin body onto his back and rubbed her furry pussy against the crease in his back.

"Hmm." Adam wiggled his toes, feeling as if he were floating on air. "This is *amazing*."

She leaned down, whispering into his ear. "It gets better."

He held his breath, nearly busting a nut on the sheet.

"Roll over."

He did, and she got on top of him again, massaging his chest while rolling her pussy against his cock.

"You like this?" She held a mischievous smile that told him she already knew he did.

"Fuck, yeah." He wiggled his erection against her. "Don't ever have to ask."

"It feels like..." She bounced, sending sharp sensations through his shaft. "You wanna fuck. Do you?"

"Again, you don't have to ask." He grinded against her moist labia but didn't enter. "I've wanted to fuck you since I saw you."

She blushed. "Do you like this position or something else?"

He loved that view of looking up at a woman's tits as she bounced on his dick, but he wanted to see that ass.

"Turn around." He narrowed his eyes. "Ride it from the other direction."

"Okay—"

"And take your hair down."

He loved pulling a woman's hair when he fucked her.

"Your wish is my command." She unwrapped her braids from the bun and flipped them over one shoulder.

"Yeah." He swallowed. "You are so beautiful."

She turned around, spread her ass cheeks apart with her hands and

sat on his dick.

"*Yes.*" Adam wrapped his hands into her braids. "That's it. Ride me, Grace."

"With pleasure—"

Her purse buzzed.

"Fuck." Adam groaned. "Your phone again."

"I...I apologize." She climbed off him and got her purse. "Sorry."

Adam sighed, scratching his balls.

"You've got to be kidding me." She read the screen. "Ten times?"

"What? Is that the same person from earlier?"

"I'm turning it off." She pressed her fingertip into the phone. "It's nothing."

"Doesn't seem like nothing. Is someone bothering you, Grace?"

"No, no." She got a condom from the basket and twisted back to the bed. "Please forget it."

"You keep walking like *that* and it'll be easy to. I love the way you walk."

She giggled, and it was the first time he noticed her dimples.

"Seriously," he said. "You can tell me if you need help."

"I'm fine, Adam. It's not your concern."

"You said it was a client earlier—"

"Please." She slipped the condom on him. "Don't ruin the mood."

"Okay." He took her hand. "Lay down."

"I thought you wanted me on top."

"Not anymore." He laid her down beside him and while stroking her braids, lost himself in her intoxicating eyes and attempted a kiss.

"No." She frowned, lifting her finger between their mouths.

Fuck it, he worked on her titty, sucking and flicking the nipple back and forth with his tongue. Sensing she was ready for him, he fondled her pussy and spread her sticky labia open.

Grace panted, catching her breath in her throat.

"Fuck foreplay." He rolled her over, mounted her and shoved his pulsating dick inside her.

She thrashed against him, grabbing at the sheets and moaning.

Her cunt made him feel like a starved, desperate dope feign who'd finally gotten his fix after stumbling around for days searching for a high. Every thrust introduced his dick to a unique sensation.

He thought his soon-to-be ex-wife Ronnie had been the best fuck he had, with drunk ass Vette a close second, but they didn't compare to Grace one bit.

"Right there, Grace." He squeezed his fingers into her soft flesh. "Oh."

Adam humped harder, the bed frame beating the wall like it was Floyd Mayweather. "Whose pussy is this, huh? Whose is it?"

"Yours."

"Who? Say my name." He yanked her braids. "Say my fucking name."

"It's yours, Adam!"

"You damn right it is." He moved faster, riding that cunt like a beast. "Say my name again. Loud!"

"Adam, yes!" She grabbed his arms, her titties bouncing from side-to-side. "Oh! Don't stop."

****

"No."

Adam awoke the next morning to Grace arguing in his bathroom. It took him a second to realize she was on the phone.

"I mean it," she said. "Leave me alone. I can't take this anymore."

Adam heard her heading out the bathroom and lay over, pretending he was still asleep. "Oh." He pretended to awake when she entered. "Hey there."

"Good morning, Adam." She glided to the bed in her dress, looking like a living portrait. "Did you sleep well?"

"The best sleep I've had in years." He stretched against the fluffy pillows. "You're dressed. Are you leaving? You promised to show me around the city today."

"I'd love to." Her white teeth gleamed. "And I shall. I have to run to my place to freshen up and then I'll be back." She gestured to her dress, grinning. "I don't want to go out in the same dress as last night."

"Why not?" He took her hand and pulled her on the bed. "You look gorgeous in it. You look even better out of it."

She set her cellphone on the nightstand.

"Let me guess. Was that the same person who called you all last night?"

"Sh." She pressed her finger to his lips.

"Mm." He put his arm around her waist. "Let me kiss you—"

"No." She jerked back. "No, Adam."

"In this moment, looking into my eyes and being this close, you're telling me you don't want to kiss me?" He inched his mouth to hers. "Come on—"

"Adam, I will leave." She pressed her lips together. "These are my rules. If you can't accept them—"

"Fine." He let her go, mumbling.

"Don't be mad." She stroked his cheek. "After this, you won't even think about a kiss." She got another condom and within moments, Grace had him hard as cement, riding his stick with animalistic fervor.

"Ah, yeah." Adam gripped her waist, bouncing her. "Yes, Grace." He pushed his back into the bed. "Yes."

The bed shrieked and squealed, shaking the nightstand off balance.

"I love your dick, Adam." She bounced harder. "You're so handsome."

He grunted. "Slow it down a bit. Ah."

If Grace's pussy had a name, it would've been "magic".

She spun her hips, gyrating and thrusting until he flooded the condom.

"Ahhhh." Adam jiggled her, draining every drop of cum into the rubber.

"Oh." She rolled over breathless, her brown body dotted in sweat. "You're so good."

He rubbed his sweaty abs. "Am I?"

"Oh, *yes*." She closed her eyes, her entire body trembling as she exhaled. "Many of my clients are horrible because they don't care about pleasing me and only getting off. But you please me, Adam."

"If you don't enjoy it then I won't." He kissed her hand. "I'm jealous."

"Jealous?"

"Of that client who keeps calling you. Guess he's hooked, huh? Can't blame him. I'm hooked now too."

"Adam." She leaned up. "You are getting confused."

"I'm not confused." He dragged his finger down her thigh. "I know exactly what I'm saying."

"I'm an escort, Adam." She swallowed. "This is just business."

"If you stay here long enough..." He held her neck, guiding her mouth to his. "It can be more—"

"No." She shook her head, pushing him away. "Please, stop, Adam."

"*Why*?" He let her go. "Why can you fuck me, bathe me, but I can't get a kiss?"

She avoided eye contact. "This is a job."

"Bullshit. How we talk, what we've shared, it's more than business."

"After one night?"

"Yes after one fuckin' night. I feel something for you, Grace. Already."

"I'll have sex with you anytime you want. Make your stay pleasurable, but we can't cross that line." She tightened her lips. "No kissing."

"Fuck that." Adam grabbed her again. He never manhandled women, but he needed to kiss her if only to make her realize this was more than a job. Or maybe convince himself it was. "Come here." He grabbed her skinny face.

"No!" She fidgeted, whimpering and shoving. "Stop it."

He let her go and slammed his head against the pillow.

"You want me to leave and not come back? Because you're acting like an animal."

He sighed into his hands.

"You say you're different than my other clients but you're acting just like them." She stood. "Like just because you pay for my time you own me. Well, you do not." She twisted to the dresser and got her ponytail holder. "I will not be disrespected."

"Fuck, Grace, I'm human. I *want* to kiss you. I'm not apologizing for that."

"What is it with you men? What women say isn't important?"

"I didn't say that."

"I don't belong to you or any man." She wrapped the ponytail holder around her hair and twisted her braids into a bun. "I am tired of men thinking they can take anything they want from me. Tired, Adam."

"All right calm down. Jeez." He straightened the pillow behind his head. "I won't do it again."

"You better not." She got her phone from the nightstand. "Or money or not, this is over."

CHAPTER SEVEN

"Hello, Grace." Sokoro Otieno greeted her when she entered her home, his voice so deep it shook the octagon tiles of her living room.

"What is this?" She yanked her key out her door before closing it. "Sokoro, what are you doing in my house?"

The 32-year-old lothario remained on her white sectional, his 6'5 body tucked into jeans and a white Gucci blazer, gold jewelry glistening from his silky, cocoa-brown skin. "I'm tired of you ignoring me."

She threw her purse on the glass coffee table. "Get out of my house or I'll call the law."

"The law?" He laughed, his perfect square teeth so white they could light up the darkness. "You forget who I am, Grace? I own the law. Everyone around here does what I say and you will be no different."

"Why are you doing this? Please, leave me alone."

"You weren't telling me to leave you alone after I gave your family that one million shillings when the white man tried to force your family off their land, were you?" He rubbed his slick, bald head, angular cheeks flexing with every word he spoke. "Weren't telling me to go away when your family needed money for food or when your mother got sick and couldn't afford her medication. What's changed?"

"We didn't know we'd made a deal with the devil."

"You should've known." He lifted his athletic frame off the couch, closing his blazer. "You refuse me, Grace? I'm royalty around here. I got women throwing themselves at my feet—"

"Then harass *them*. I won't nothing to do with you, Sokoro. Leave me and my family alone or you will be sorry."

His cackle rattled through her, shaking the walls. "Oh, that's what I love about you, Grace. Your spunk. Not that your beauty isn't more than enough to keep a man satisfied and your uh..." He walked his stare down her body. "Your other attributes. Should I mention them?"

"You'll never have me, Sokoro."

"Is that, right? Oh, wait. I had you already." He winked. "More than once. Did you forget?"

"You had my body." She stuck her chin in the air. "Not my heart. That you'll never get no matter how much money you have or how many times you threaten my family."

"I wouldn't be so sure." He straightened his sleeve. "Either your family pays the debt they owe for me saving that godforsaken dump of a village, or you marry me." His wide smile took up his entire face. "Simple as that."

"Never!"

"Come on, Grace. Let me make an honest woman out of you. You can't like slinging your body to every tourist that comes into town."

"I'd rather fuck every scoundrel on this earth than to be with you. You don't even need the money, Sokoro. You do this to torture us. To show you're in control."

"So because I'm well off, I don't deserve my money back?" He shook his head, clicking his jaw. "What world are you living in, Grace? You expect thousands for free and me get nothing? I'm not even asking for all the other times your sniveling joke of a father came begging me for money."

"Stop it." She got on her tiptoes but didn't reach anywhere close to his face. "My father is an honorable man. Ten times the man you'll ever be."

"So honorable he can't even support his family? Living in that pigsty village? Is that what you want to go back to, Grace?" He frowned. "The bush? Bathing with the same animals you eat? Drinking their feces? You want to live like an animal?"

"Don't you ever talk about my family that way. We are proud people!"

"So proud that your parents pimp their daughter out for money?"

She raised her hand to slap him, but he grabbed it.

"Uh-uh." He squinted his espresso-brown eyes. "You'd better think about that real quick, Sweetheart. Let's not get violent, Grace. You won't win that fight."

"Let me go!" She snatched her hand free.

"Marry me."

"You don't have to force a woman into marriage." She rubbed her aching wrist. "You're gorgeous and rich. You could have any woman you want."

"And I want *you*. Why is that so hard for you to understand?"

She rocked. "I'll get you the money myself."

He laughed. "You gonna suck every dick in Nairobi? Because that's what it will take for you to raise what your family owes me. You're doing well for yourself Grace, but not *that* well." He walked around her living room of slate-blue walls and icy-gray tile floor. "This is a beautiful home, but we know it wasn't easy for the village girl to come up. How do you think you rented this place, Grace?"

"With the money I make." She grimaced. "How the fuck do you think?"

"You have no credit." He walked behind the couch, massaging the back of it as he did. "Even with what you make, how do you think you got a deal on a place like this in this neiGHForhood?"

She held her breath.

"Me, Grace." He walked across the rug to the connecting kitchen. "I got this place for you."

"Liar! I bought this with *my* money."

"Because I spoke to the owner."

She shook, gritting her teeth. "You're lying."

"Course he's no longer the owner." He got the carton of orange juice out of the refrigerator.

"What are you talking about?"

Sokoro stared at her as he drank. "Ah." He set the glass on the counter. "I own this house now. I bought it last week. Hello, Grace." He grinned. "Meet your new landlord."

"Filthy liar. You're lying to manipulate me."

"It is true." He walked out the kitchen, approaching her. "You can't get away from me, Grace. I own you just like I do this property. Now..." He caressed her shoulders as she fought not to vomit. "You can be a smart girl and realize all a life with me offers or you can go back to the bush and bathe with the rhinos. Of course, if your family doesn't repay me, your village will be gone and your family dead—"

"Sokoro." She covered her mouth, gasping. "Please leave my family alone. I beg you."

"Oh, Grace." He took off her head wrap and pushed his nose into her braids. "That's the deal. You do what I want or suffer the consequences."

"No." She punched his chest as he strangled her in his embrace. "I'll get you the money. Leave my family alone!"

"You'll get me the money?"

"Yes." She sobbed. "Yes!"

"Okay." He pulled her head back. "But I need some collateral." He unbuckled his belt with his free hand.

"No." She squeezed her eyes shut. "No, Sokoro."

"Sh." He lowered her on her knees as she trembled. "Be a good girl, Grace. Show your appreciation for all I've done."

"No, please." He held her head still as he unzipped his pants. "No!"

CHAPTER EIGHT

"Trust me, Adam." Grace accompanied Adam from his hotel room a few hours later. "I'll show you all Nairobi can offer."

"Sounds great but are you all right? You seem like something is on your mind."

"I'm fine." She smiled, yet Adam wasn't convinced. "We'll go everywhere. Let me see." Her eyes lit up as she clasped her hands, bracelets jiggling. "You like animals?"

"I love animals."

"Great. We'll go to the National Park and the Safari Walk."

"Sounds nice." He didn't care if they visited a dump as long as he could spend the day with Grace.

They walked downstairs. Grace's dress brushed the steps as her sandals held her delicate feet. "We'll go to the Karen Blixen Museum too. You'll love it!"

"Who is Karen Blixen?"

"*Adam.*" She groaned and even that sounded sexy. "Karen Blixen is the author of *Out of Africa*. Remember the movie with Meryl Streep and Robert Redford?"

"I remember the movie but didn't know it was a book." He laughed as they got to the first floor.

"The book is even better than the movie. It's the story of Karen's life in Africa." She stuck her skinny finger in the air. "You should read it. I'm a true romantic and that book blew me away."

"*You* blow me away."

Grace dipped her head, redness caressing her brown cheeks. "You are sweet."

"And you're amazing."

"Ah, Mr. Adam." Meshack rocked behind the front desk with a smile as wide as Canada. "Good day. Did you sleep well?"

"Very well." Adam stood at the counter, winking at Grace, who rolled her eyes with a snicker. "Everything's perfect."

"Well, I'm glad to hear that," Meshack said. "Grace is a sweetie and tourists love her. She knows the city well and will take care of you."

"I will." She batted her sweeping lashes.

Adam rubbed up against her. "And I want to be taken care *of*."

"Well, well, well," Vette walked down the stairs. "What do we have here?" She stopped in front of Grace and Adam with resting bitch face. "And you are?"

"I'm Grace." Grace bowed, holding her hand out to her. "It's nice to meet you."

Vette glared at her hand and then at Adam. "And where did he find you?"

Grace grimaced, pulling her hand back. "He didn't *find* me anywhere."

"Grace is a tour guide." Adam took Grace's arm. "I found her on the Internet. She's gonna show me around the city."

"Do I look stupid to you?" Vette crossed her arms. "If she's a tour guide than I'm your mother."

"Then we'll be seeing you, 'Mom.'" Adam rolled his eyes as he pulled Grace away toward the door. "We have things to do."

"So I'm not invited?" Vette scoffed.

"I invited you to see the sights yesterday. You didn't want to." Adam opened the door for Grace. "After you."

"You're just leaving me here?" Vette yelled. "What the fuck am I supposed to do?"

A passing woman gasped at the vulgarity.

"You're a resourceful woman, Vette." Adam winked. "I'm sure you'll find some way to entertain yourself." He helped Grace out the door.

"Who was that?" Grace asked as they exited the front steps.

"Nobody."

She faced him, fixing her purse on her shoulder. "She likes you."

He nodded, taking a stick of gum from his pocket. "How do you know?"

"I'm a woman." She patted his cheek. "We know *everything*."

CHAPTER NINE

Grace promised Adam a hell of a time and she did not disappoint. She showed Adam places he'd never heard of and the more Adam saw, the more curious he got. His heart warmed at every stop and he could feel why they called Africa "The Motherland". It wasn't just for black heritage, but Africa had lent so much of its beauty and authenticity to the American way of life that it was impossible for Adam not to be thankful.

After touring Ngong Hills, Grace took Adam to a two-story restaurant made of bamboo walls and decorated with East African artifacts. Striking waitresses strutted around in vibrant, multi-colored head wraps that matched their dresses.

Adam and Grace got an outside table where they could see the overlapping mountains in the distance.

Nairobi was unlike any place Adam had been because every experience was a part of its culture. The aroma of curry powder and strong native spices tickled his nose. The restaurant alone told Adam everything he needed to know about the city.

Grace ordered them beef curry along with her favorite and a very common Kenyan dish; Ugali, a porridge made of maize flour.

Food looked like a painting on the plates; bright, lively and rich with a variety of heat and spices which made Adam feel like he tasted African culture with each bite.

"You said this was super food." Adam chewed. "What makes it super?"

Grace sipped from her glass of apple juice with a straw. "Because it's my favorite."

He laughed. "That makes sense."

"Why? Do you not like it?"

"No, I love it. It's delicious. I love the spices. Don't tell my mom, but this is the best cooking I've ever had."

Grace smiled while chewing. "I grew up on this food."

"Are you a good cook?"

"Of course." She bounced, sitting back. "All Nairobi women can cook. It is a big part of our culture. Cooking is how we show love to our family. You should taste my cooking."

Adam rubbed the toe of his sneaker against her leg. "There's something else of yours I'd love to taste."

"I'm serious." She chuckled, swatting his foot away. "You should let me cook for you."

"I'd love that but might not have enough time."

"Oh." She dropped her stare to the table. "How long will you be in the city? I forgot to ask."

"A few more days."

Her face fell.

"Why?" His heart fluttered. "You hoping it will be more?"

She lifted her chin, shaking her shoulders. "No."

He didn't buy that one bit. She was starting to become attached to him as much as he had her.

The umbrellas above their heads, which shielded customers from the sun, shifted a bit in the muggy breeze.

Grace giggled, wincing.

"What?" Adam drank some of his tangy pineapple juice. "Why are you giggling?"

"It's you." She covered her mouth as she chewed. "You keep staring at me."

"Well, you're a beautiful woman."

"Stop." She laughed under her hand. "I don't want you watching me eat. Look at the mountains."

He turned his head away for a second then faced her again. "Nah, I'm good."

She snickered, wiping her mouth.

"You're amazing, Grace. You deserve the world."

"Many men have promised that to me." She waved her fork, swallowing. "But I don't want a man to give me anything, Adam."

"I doubt that." He sat back. "What about love? Don't you want *that*?"

"Romantic love is an illusion." She drew lines in her food with her fork. "At least for people like me."

"That's ridiculous. You telling me you've never been in love?"

"Where I come from, love is a luxury I can't afford. Other things take precedence. Like survival."

"So? Love has nothing to do with where we come from or what we've gone through. If love is coming, it's coming. We have no power over Cupid's arrow. If we did, we wouldn't let ourselves be so tortured by relationships or allow our hearts to be torn into shreds. People can't control love. It controls *you*. Plus, it always comes when you least expect it."

He caught the glimmer in her eye, which suggested she'd gotten the hint that he might've been talking about *them*.

"You've had a special love?" she asked. "One more important than the others?"

"Ronnie." He wiggled his mouth. "Veronica. My wife."

"Wife?" Grace gaped. "You're married?"

"Separated." He squeezed his cup. "About seven months."

"What happened?"

"She fell out of love with me." He shrugged, eyes watering. "Met a guy at her job who swept her off her feet and paid more attention to her than she felt I did."

"Is that true?"

"Guess so." His voice cracked from emotion. "I put all my time into the GHF, and I didn't realize Ronnie felt like she was just waiting on the sidelines. She thought I'd pull further away from the organization, but I got more into it. It put a huge strain on our marriage, me traveling all the time, but I love doing this and helping people."

Grace smiled.

"I love knowing I did something to make someone's life better."

She patted his hand. "I'm sorry, Adam. It's her loss."

"She loves someone else. It is what it is."

"Do you still love her?"

"I'll always love Ronnie. Once you're married, that person becomes a part of you. But we don't belong together and I accept that. I just want her to be happy. Besides, in all the time I've been with Ronnie, I've never felt like this."

Grace squeezed his hand. "To new beginnings, aye?"

"Exactly." Adam stared into her glowing eyes. "And I'm ready for them."

CHAPTER TEN

Adam followed Grace upstairs to his hotel room, enjoying every swivel of her body.

She turned from the door, blushing when she caught his stare. "I had a wonderful day, Adam. The most fun I've had in a long time."

"Don't you do this with all your clients?"

"Yes." She'd taken her head wrap off and was now playing with it in her hands. "But it never felt like this."

"Like what?" He leaned against the door, moving closer to her.

"I don't know." She dropped her head.

"You know." He lifted her chin. "You feel what I feel. Something you don't understand but you love it all the same."

"I'll come back tonight." She stepped back from the door. "Do you like to dance?"

"I like anything if I do it with you."

"There's a club I like to go to. It's not fancy, but I want to take you there. We'll have fun."

"I'd love that."

She turned to leave, and he put his arm around her waist. "I'm not done with you yet."

She tucked in her lips. "Is that so?"

He unlocked the door and pulled her over the threshold.

"What is this?"

He pushed her against the door. "This is me taking control." He kissed down her dress, pulling it up as he got on his knees.

She moaned, her head wrap slipping from her fingers.

Adam took off her white thong and sniffed the sweet, womanly scent of her bush, widening her legs until his tongue met her clit.

"Mm." Grace threw her leg over his shoulder, rocking as licked her labia. "Oh, Adam." She rubbed her tits, the end of her dress tickling his head. "Ooh."

59

He didn't lick hard, just tickled her clit with the tip of his tongue.

She gyrated, squeezing his head between her thighs.

He turned his head sideways, getting his tongue further inside her, his dick rising when he saw the pink walls of her vagina.

"Uh-huh." She ran her fingers through his hair. "Please don't stop, Adam."

He sucked until she released, drowning his tongue.

"Oh." Grace went limp, falling over as he held her. "Jesus."

He stood, swooped her into his arms and threw her on the bed face first.

"What are you gonna do?" she mumbled into the bedspread.

"You scared?" He panted, taking off his belt.

"No."

He bounded her wrists with his belt and pulled them over her head. "Don't move." He yanked up her dress, tearing the thin material on one side.

She gasped. "You tore it."

He grinned. "You won't care after this."

Adam kissed around her tight buttocks and spread them, sticking his tongue in her tight asshole.

"Oh, yes." She writhed. "Yes, Adam. My ass. Yes!"

He moaned as he sucked her anus, shocked even that part tasted good. Ass eating disgusted him before he met Ronnie. But after years of her begging him to rim her, he finally had and it had quickly become one of his favorite acts.

He'd thank Ronnie later.

"There!" Grace lifted her head. "Right there, Adam. Oh, I'm coming."

He spit on her ass and spread the moisture from her asshole all the way to her pussy. "God, I want you so bad." He pulled his zipper down so hard he almost tore it. "I'm gonna fuck you in the ass, Grace."

She writhed.

"Is that okay?"

"Yes but get a condom." She wiggled her hips. "Adam."

"I got this." He grabbed his pack of Magnums from his pants.

"Let me see it." She struggled to look over her shoulder and he realized she didn't trust him.

He showed it to her.

"Okay." She sighed, nodding.

"You don't trust me?"

"It's just that some men pretend to wear them and I can't tell."

"Grace." He caressed her side. "I'd never, ever do something so shitty."

She flashed a smile over her shoulder. "I know."

Not wanting the awkward conversation to kill the mood, Adam tore the condom open with his teeth, and slid it on his shaft. "You ready?"

"Yes, yes!" She pushed her face to the bed. "Fuck me, Adam."

He spread her cheeks so wide he could see her little hole pulsating. It had widened since he'd sucked it. To his surprise, it took a minimal amount of tugging and he was inside her. As he pumped, her ass clenched his shaft, squeezing every nerve.

"Yeah." He pulled her arms toward him, yanking the belt as he fucked her. "Ah." Her ass smothered his dick while wetness seeped from her pussy. "You're so wet, Grace. Ah."

"Yes." She bounced her head as he pounded her so hard their skin made slapping noises. "Ooh. Oh!"

Adam pumped, face drowning in sweat. "Grace. Oh!"

Also by Stacy-Deanne

Billionaires For Black Girls
Billionaire for the Night
Billionaire Takes the Bride
Billionaire At 36k Feet
Billionaire's Love Trap
Billionaire in the Caribbean
Billionaire Broken
Billionaire Times Two

Sex in the Wild West Series
Maid for Two
Fling on the Frontier
Favor for His Wife
The Carriage Ride
The Bride in the Barn
The Guest of Honor
Sunday Meal

Stripped Romantic Suspense Series
Stripped

Captured

Damaged

Haunted

Possessed

Destined

Stripped Series (Books 1-5)

Stripped Series Books 1-3

Stripped Series (Books 4-6)

Tate Valley Romantic Suspense Series

Now or Never

Now or Never

Chasing Forever

Chasing Forever

Sinner's Paradise

Sinner's Paradise

Last Dance

Last Dance

Tate Valley The Complete Series

The Bruised Series

Bruised

Captivated

Disturbed

Entangled

Twisted

The Good Girls and Bad Boys Series

Who's That Girl?
You Know My Name
Hate the Game

The Studs of Clear Creek County
The White Knight Cowboy
The Forlorn Cowboy
The Lavish Cowboy

Standalone
The Seventh District
Gonna Make You Mine
Empty
Gonna Make You Mine
Protecting Her Lover
What Grows in the Garden
Love is a Crime
On the Way to Heaven
Open Your Heart
Open Your Heart
A Matter of Time
Hero
Outside Woman
The Watchers
Harm a Fly
Harm a Fly
An Unexpected Love
You're the One
Worth the Risk
Hawaii Christmas Baby

The Best Christmas Ever
Prey
The Good Girls and Bad Boys Series
Bruised Complete Series
Tate Valley Complete Series
The Princess and the Thief
The Little Girl
The Stranger
Oleander
Seducing Her Father's Enemy
Love & Murder: 3-Book Romantic Suspense Starter Set
Paradise
Stalked by the Quarterback
Stripped Complete Series
Tell Me You Love Me
Secrets of the Heart
Five Days
Off the Grid
Sex in Kenya
Fatal Deception
A Cowboy's Debt
Billionaires for Black Girls Set (1-4)
A Savior for Christmas
The Samsville Setup
Trick The Treat
The Cowboy She Left in Wyoming
Theodore's Ring
Wrangle Me, Cowboy
The Billionaire's Slave
The Cowboy's Twin
Everwood County Plantation
Billionaires for Black Girls Set 5-7
The Lonely Hearts of San Sity

Stranded with Billionaire Grumpy Pants